For Jennifer Hochhauser
—H.Z.

ISBN 0-439-23226-2

12 11 10 9 8 7 6 5 4 3 2 1 1 2 3 4 5/0
Printed in China for PUBLISHING PARTNERS.
Bandages made in Japan
First Scholastic printing, February 2001.

always, Melissa

Harriet Ziefert

Friends Stick Together

drawings by Rebecca Doughty

SCHOLASTIC INC.

New York Toronto London Auckland Sydney Mexico City New Delhi Hong Kong

Sometimes it's okay

if she takes more than half.

mine

yours

U CAMEL!

A bandage can make a big difference.

Remember
her favorite
color
is purple.
ya baby!

Save a place in line.

Be patient when she tells the same story
you
K & S,
K & S...
me
for the fifth time.

cell phone

If your friend loses a ~~sneaker~~,
help her look for it.

If you've already said you can't go,
don't show up with someone else.

Share your umbrella.

Don't say,

"The last one there is a rotten egg!"

It's good to have something in your lunch bag to share.

Your backpack may be nicer,

but you don't need to say so.

you
me
me
you
stick up for your friend.

Don't call her dog ugly,
or mean, or stupid.

Don't squeeze her guinea pig.

Don't be a copycat.

AVRIL

AVRIL

You can't start over

just because you're losing.

Share your nail polish.

Don't expect your friend to be excited when you get "100".

Don't put sprinkles on her ice cream

if she prefers pickles.

Exchange hats on the way to school.

Half the fun of pizza is sharing it.

Don't make fun
of her new hairdo.
BENSON

Collect things together.
always keep knees down

Being captain doesn't mean you're the best or the smartest.

play, don't just watch.

BUS
STOP
If she has to wear boots, don't laugh.

If the ~~horse~~ KUD she's drawing looks more like a cow, don't say anything.

KUD

oo-ch-ah
oo-ch-ah
oo-ch-ah
Sometimes you just clap.

Hold hands, then jump in together.

If she trips, help her get up.

Friends stick together.

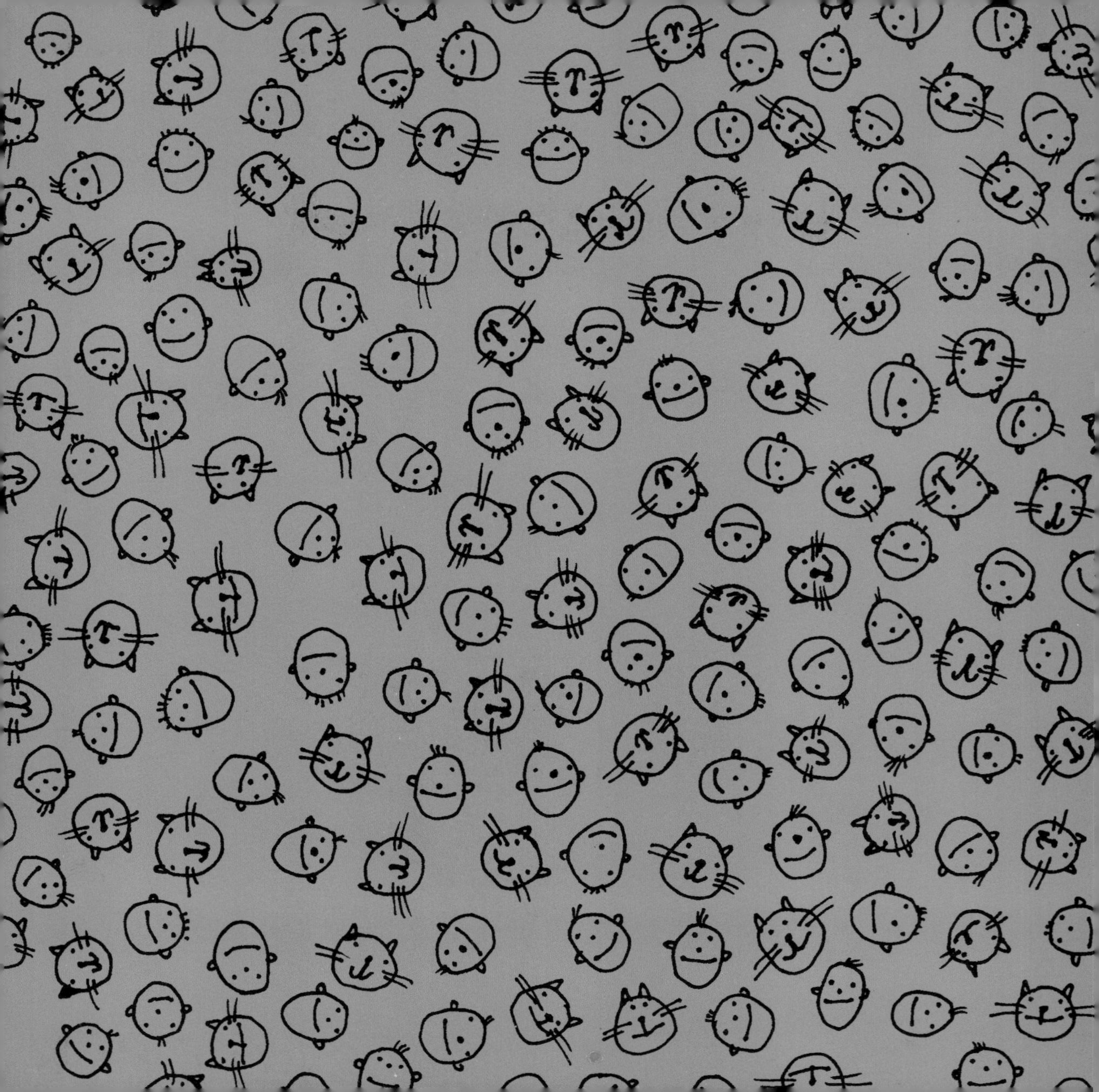